Loved Her Enough to Lose Myself

I broke every bond to keep her — and she left me with none.

"Based on true story"

By

Raghavan Adhisankar

Loved Her Enough to Lose Myself
I broke every bond to keep her — and she left me with none.

This is a work of nonfiction. The events and experiences described are based on the real-life journey of the author. Certain names have been changed to respect privacy, but the emotional truth of this story remains entirely intact.

Published by Self-published by the Author
First Edition: 2025

ISBN: 978-93-343-2754-0

Cover Design by the Author
Interior Design by the Author

For permissions or inquiries, contact:
raghavanadhisankar@gmail.com

Printed in India.

CHAPTERS

STORY SUMMARY

In a quiet South Indian village where tradition clings tightly to its people, Rumplestiltskin lives a life defined by duty. A husband, a father, a provider—he performs his roles with silent acceptance. His world is stable, but numb; his heart has long forgotten the language of longing. Until one fateful evening, when a quiet girl named Belle crosses his path and awakens something ancient within him.

She is not glamorous. She is not loud. But in her eyes, Rumplestiltskin sees reflection—of all that he has lost, and all he still yearns to become. What begins as a spark in a passing glance soon deepens into a hidden universe, shared only in stolen moments, whispered words, and the kind of vulnerability that unnerves even the strongest of men.

But love in a village like his comes at a cost. The price? Everything. His reputation. His family. The trust he once held in his own reflection. Rumplestiltskin is forced to choose between the comfort of a predictable life and the chaos of a love that promises to make him whole. Belle, too, stands at a crossroads—between a life chosen for her and a man who sees her for who she truly is.

As their bond deepens, secrets unravel and the village begins to whisper. The choices they make threaten to shatter not only their lives but everyone around them. Yet through heartbreak, betrayal, sacrifice, and unbearable longing, one truth remains: the undeniable, irreplaceable force of a love born in truth, nurtured in defiance, and tested by time.

Loved Her Enough to Lose Myself is not just a love story. It is a story of souls colliding, of pain endured in silence, of loyalty in the face of betrayal, and of a man who gave up everything for the woman who walked away—leaving him with a heart full of memories, and a name she never truly let go.

DEDICATION

For the one who walked away —

and for the man who never stopped waiting.

This is for you, Belle.

And for the version of me who loved you enough to lose myself.

ACKNOWLEDGEMENT

To every soul who walked beside me in the shadows —

Your presence gave me the strength to face another day.

To those who stood by me when the world turned away —

your faith will never be forgotten.

To my readers — if you see yourself in these pages,

know that you are not alone.

And to Belle — wherever life has taken you,

This story carries the echo of what we once were.

Preface

This is not a tale told in fiction.

It is memory, written down before it could disappear.

You may see pain in these pages.

But behind every line is a man who once believed love could save anything.

If you've ever stayed quiet when your heart screamed,

if you've ever let someone go just to keep them happy,

if you've ever been broken — but still prayed for them…

Then this story is yours, too.

Read it slowly.

Not to understand.

But to remember.

Author's Note

I didn't write this book to be read.

I wrote it because I needed to bleed somewhere.

Each page — is not fiction.

It is where I lived.

What I loved.

And what I lost.

I once gave everything I had —

not for fame, not for recognition,

but for one person.

I stood by her against the world,

only to be left standing alone.

But if you ask me today:

"Would you do it again?"

My answer is simple: Yes.

Because when I loved her, I loved her completely.

Even in her betrayal… she remained the one I prayed for.

I wrote this for those who gave too much.

For those whose silence was louder than any scream.

You are not weak.

You are not alone.

If even one word in these pages belongs to you —

then none of this was in vain.

— Raghavan Adhisankar

Prologue

There are nights when I still hear her voice.

Not in words — in the silence between them.

There are mornings when my hands reach out, forgetting they are meant to be empty now.

We spend our lives thinking time will soften the sharp edges of memory.

But some memories were never meant to dull.

Some loves were never meant to fade.

This is not a story I chose to tell.

It is a story that would not let me remain silent.

So if you choose to turn these pages — know this:

You are walking through a heart that was broken, rebuilt, and broken again.

And somewhere, in these words — a man still waits for a woman who may never return.

CHAPTER 1
THE FIRST SPARK

Chapter 1: The First Spark

The night lay still—one of those village nights when even the wind forgets to move, and time seems to sigh beneath the weight of memories not yet made. The stars blinked behind a soft veil of moonlight. Somewhere far off, a koel called through the darkness, its song dipping in and out of the silence like a secret. The air was heavy with jasmine, sweet and ancient, like it had been hanging there since the gods first whispered stories into the earth.

Rumplestiltskin stood by the corner tea stall, fingers wrapped loosely around a lukewarm glass of half-drunk chai. He wasn't waiting for anyone. Not anymore. Life, for him, had become a path he didn't choose—only followed. Each day is measured in duties. Each night swallowed by silence. His laughter, long forgotten. His wants, carefully buried beneath responsibilities that wore his name like chains.

And then... she appeared.

Not like a storm. Not like a song.

She came like a breath.

Belle.

She didn't arrive to be seen, but she was impossible to miss.

A maroon salwar clung softly to her frame, and a loose dupatta trailed behind her like it belonged to the wind. Her long braid swung with each step—deliberate, graceful, unaware. Her gaze stayed low, not out of shyness, but a practiced defiance. A woman used to move through a world that looked but never truly saw.

Rumplestiltskin's hand stilled.

His chest clenched.

And for a moment, the earth forgot to spin.

His heart didn't pound — it staggered.

Not fast. But heavy. Like something sacred had stirred inside him for the first time in years.

She walked past him, unhurried. As if she had walked past him a hundred times in another life.

And just as she crossed, her eyes flicked up — for a second.

A single second.

Brown. Soft. Tired. Honest.

And gone.

There were no words. No sparks flying from the sky.

But something had already caught fire.

That night, Rumplestiltskin sat on the edge of his cot, his feet flat on the cold cement floor, staring at nothing — and feeling everything.

He wasn't a boy. He wasn't reckless.

He knew what it was to be attracted, to be tempted.

But this was none of that.

This was... recognition.

He didn't even know her name.

He hadn't heard her voice.

But something inside him—something he thought was long dead—had moved.

And that was enough.

He knew her walk.

He knew the sound of her footsteps as they faded into the night.

And above all, he knew—without logic, without warning—his life had just changed.

CHAPTER 2
A LOVE AGAINST ALL ODDS

Chapter 2: A Love Against All Odds

Some stories begin with logic.

Others with fate.

But theirs began in defiance—against time, against society, against every rule carved into stone.

After that single passing moment on the moonlit street, Rumplestiltskin found himself walking through the village not with purpose, but with hope. Hope that she'd appear again—not like a miracle, not like a dream—but like a quiet answer to the question his heart had been asking for years.

He never admitted it. Not to anyone. Not even to himself.

But every bend in the road became a prayer.

Every turn, a silent longing: Let it be her.

And fate, sometimes merciful, listened.

One dusky evening, as the sky melted into a sleepy orange and the air hung thick with the scent of fresh rain and dust, he saw her again.

This time, she wasn't walking. She was still.

Laughing beside a roadside tailor shop, her eyes creased in joy, her hand brushing a friend's shoulder.

She hadn't seen him. She didn't know she was being watched.

And he—he didn't move.

He just stood there. Watching.

Not like a man watching a woman.

But like a soul watching something it had been missing for lifetimes.

Her laugh wasn't loud.

But to him, it echoed through the years he had lost.

It wasn't love yet.

It wasn't even a connection.

But it stirred something far more dangerous.

It stirred belief.

Their next meeting didn't belong to fate.

It belonged to the rituals of the family—a cousin's wedding.

The courtyard was bright with lights, loud with laughter, and suffocating with relatives.

And yet, in the middle of it all, she arrived—wrapped in a soft green saree, jasmine woven through her braid, her face glowing not with makeup, but with quiet dignity.

Their eyes met. Across the noise. Across the chaos.

This time, she didn't look away.

This time, she saw him.

What followed wasn't fast.

It was slow. Careful. Hidden.

It was the kind of beginning that blooms in the shadows—subtle glances at temple events, polite smiles that held too much weight, and words exchanged in public spaces that meant everything in private.

It wasn't built on rebellion.

It wasn't even romantic—at first.

It was built on something rarer.

Understanding.

He told her things he'd never told another soul.

Of what it felt like to return home and feel invisible.

Of what it meant to meet everyone's expectations but never be truly seen.

Of carrying the title of father, husband, provider—and feeling like none of them fit anymore.

And Belle listened.

Not like someone curious.

Not like someone impressed.

But like someone who had waited her whole life to hear words she never had permission to say aloud.

She spoke, too. Slowly. Gently.

Of dreams so simple they hurt to hear—

To become a teacher.

To be respected.

To be loved not for what she did, but for who she was.

She spoke of being raised to be obedient, not opinionated.

Of a life built by others, not by herself.

And for the first time, someone told her she deserved more.

Not in grand speeches. Not with promises.

But in every moment he looked at her like she mattered.

He didn't bring her flowers.

He brought her validation.

And that was more dangerous than anything else.

And soon... the world noticed.

Villages see everything.

And they speak before they understand.

Why was Belle smiling more?

Why did Rumplestiltskin start lingering near the bus stand longer than usual?

Then one night, the truth came in a whisper.

A phone call. Her voice, trembling.

"My brother found my messages..."

"They took my phone. They're planning my wedding next month."

He felt his world tilt, but his voice remained calm.

"If you want… I'll walk away," he said.

"I won't let them destroy your life because of me."

The silence was long.

Too long.

Then her voice, broken yet stronger than ever:

"Even if they tie me to someone else… my soul will stay with you."

That night, he didn't walk home.

He drifted—through the house, past the faces that no longer felt like family.

Past his wife. Past his children.

Through the walls of a life he no longer recognized as his own.

And for the first time... he didn't feel guilty.

Because for the first time in decades,

He wasn't surviving.

He was living.

CHAPTER 3
TWO LIVES, ONE HEART

Chapter 3: Two Lives, One Heart

There was no name for what lived between them.

No label that could contain it, no word that could explain it.

He was a husband. She was someone's daughter.

Two lives separated by duty—yet breathing from the same heart.

They didn't meet often.

Not because they didn't want to.

But because in a village like theirs, even the wind had ears.

A glance could turn into a rumour.

A smile, a scandal.

But distance didn't silence what was blooming between them.

It only made it burn deeper. Hotter.

Unspoken.

A phone call at dusk.

A passing glance near the market.

A message written in metaphors.

These weren't gestures—they were lifelines.

Tiny stolen moments stitched together into something sacred.

Rumplestiltskin had lived a full life. Or so he thought.

Until this—until her.

Every breath he took before her now felt like survival.

With her, he felt alive.

He would lie awake at night, not from restlessness—but to stay within the echo of her voice.

The rhythm of her laughter played in his mind like a lullaby he didn't dare fall asleep to.

It wasn't infatuation. It wasn't lust.

It was a rediscovery of something ancient—something he never thought he was allowed to feel again.

And Belle?

She wasn't just falling in love.

She was discovering herself—in his presence, in his silence, in his eyes.

In the space between his words, she found her own name.

For the first time in her life, she wasn't being told what to be.

She was being seen.

She started writing.

Not to him—but for herself.

Pages of emotions she couldn't voice aloud.

Letters she folded and hid like secret prayers beneath her clothes, between the pages of school books, under her pillow.

One note simply read:

"You don't know what you've done to me.

You made me feel like I deserve love.

Like I'm not invisible.

Even if this ends in silence… I'll remember your voice as the first time I heard it myself."

They were not reckless.

They were careful.

Too careful.

But the heart isn't built to love halfway.

And love... doesn't obey caution.

One night, under a sky dappled with stars, on a deserted rooftop drenched in shadows, Rumplestiltskin reached for her hand.

Not to pull her closer.

Not to claim her.

But to anchor her.

To remind her that even in a world designed to shame what they shared, this—what they had—was real.

Belle cried.

Not from fear.

But from disbelief.

That someone like him—tired, worn, married—could be so gentle with the broken, buried pieces of her soul.

That night, Rumplestiltskin knew something with painful clarity:

He wasn't living a double life.

He was living two truths.

One that the world saw.

And the other—the one that pulsed in secret, fragile and wild—

was the only one that truly mattered.

The one that beat inside her heart.

CHAPTER 4
THE TRUTH I TOLD HER

Chapter 4: The Truth I Told Her

There comes a moment in every forbidden love story—

A moment when truth knocks softly, yet echoes louder than lies ever could.

A moment when everything tender must face everything real.

Rumplestiltskin had arrived at that moment.

For weeks, he had lived in the glow of Belle's belief. Her eyes saw him, not as the world did—but as the man he wished he could've always been.

And that made the truth heavier.

He had hidden it, not out of cruelty, but cowardice.

Not to deceive, but to delay the shattering.

But love that is born in shadow must step into the light—

Or be lost forever.

They met where they always did—

A forgotten stone bench behind the village library, where bougainvillea spilled like old secrets, and no one came looking for either of them.

The air carried the scent of dust, leaves, and quiet anticipation.

Belle smiled first.

She always did.

From the knot of her dupatta, she untied a small piece of

jaggery candy and held it out like an offering.

He didn't take it.

That was the first silence.

And then came the second.

He looked at her—not her beauty, not her innocence, but her belief.

He looked at the *faith* in her eyes. The certainty that he was who she thought he was.

And then… he broke it.

"I need to tell you something," he said.

His voice wasn't trembling. It was worse—steady.

Steady like grief that had long made peace with guilt.

Belle tilted her head, expecting nothing dangerous.

She didn't know the ground was already crumbling beneath her.

"I'm married," he said.

The words hung in the air like smoke—sharp, slow, and impossible to swallow.

He watched the shift in her.

A blink that didn't come.

A breath that didn't finish.

She froze—not like a statue, but like someone in a dream they couldn't wake from.

"And I have… two daughters," he added. "They're little."

Still, she didn't speak.

Still, she didn't move.

She just *watched him*. As if replaying every memory, wondering if the truth had always been hiding in plain sight.

He waited for the collapse.

But Belle didn't collapse.

Her voice, when it came, was quiet—barely a whisper:

"Does your wife know about me?"

He shook his head.

That was when the tears came.

Not in rage. Not in sobs.

Just a single, steady tear that carved a slow path down her cheek—like truth itself, choosing its own way down.

But then... she did the unimaginable.

She turned toward him, eyes still wet, and said—softly, sincerely:

"I'm glad you told me.

I would've hated to fall deeper and find out too late."

No blame.

No drama.

Just devastation wrapped in dignity.

He had expected the worst—

A scream. A slap. A storm.

But Belle…

Belle was not like the world.

She didn't love him for the man he pretended to be.

She loved him for the silence he carried.

For the pain he never spoke of.

For making her feel *visible* in a world that had only ever seen through her.

She stood up.And so did he.

"I need time," she said.

Her voice didn't shake.

But her silence did.

"I'm not leaving," she added. "Not yet."

And then she walked away.

Not in shame.

Not in anger.

But in silence so full, it felt like a song.

He sat back down on the stone bench, his chest thundering

half terrified, half relieved.she knew.

And she was still there.

For now.

CHAPTER 5

The Day I Chose Her

Chapter 5: The Day I Chose Her

The day didn't come with noise.

No grand goodbye.

No thunder, no thunderclap, no applause.

Only silence.

A silence so deep, it felt like the village itself was holding its breath.

It had rained the night before. The earth was still damp, the leaves dripping quietly. And everything smelled like wet mud and unspoken truths.

Rumplestiltskin sat by the gate of his home—the same home he had built with duty, lived in with discipline, and filled with every version of himself but the true one.

He stared at the rusting nameplate that had once meant pride.

Now, it just meant a lie.

A decision had been forming inside him. Not through rage. Not through rebellion.

But through clarity.

He had tried.

I tried to live in both worlds.

A father in daylight. A lover in the shadows.

A man halved, carved, stretched.

But no soul can survive when it's split down the middle.

And Belle?

Belle had never demanded.

She had never asked him to leave. Never begged him to stay.

She had just... believed in him.

Stood quietly at a distance and loved him with the kind of patience that breaks a man more than anger ever could.

And suddenly, that belief felt heavier than everything he had ever carried.

He knew what choosing her meant.

It meant unchoosing everything else.

His wife.

His children.

His house.

His name.

His place in a village that whispered more than it forgave.

But for the first time in years—he wasn't afraid of loss.

Because for the first time—he saw himself.

Not in a mirror. Not in a title.

But in the reflection of her eyes.

That afternoon, the house was alive with the sound of everything that had nothing to do with him.

His daughters were giggling in the bedroom, arguing over something that wouldn't matter tomorrow.

His wife was in the kitchen, making tea, humming a tune she no longer noticed she sang.

Life was moving forward—as if the man in the house had never already left it in his heart.

Rumplestiltskin stood in the hallway.

"I need to speak to you," he said.

His voice wasn't angry. It wasn't loud.

It was steady, the kind of steady that comes when the decision has already been made.

His wife turned. She didn't look surprised.

Maybe she had seen it in his eyes.

Maybe she had felt it long before he found the courage to say it.

"I can't do this anymore," he whispered.

He didn't defend himself.

Didn't explain.

Didn't beg for forgiveness.

Because there is no version of this truth that doesn't wound someone.

His wife didn't cry.

She just... nodded.

Like someone who had been standing on a sinking ship far too long, and finally stopped fighting the waves.

He packed a small bag.

No jewelry.

No keepsakes.

No documents.

No photo frames.

Not even the gold ring he once swore meant forever.

He left the house with nothing—except the belief that maybe...

Maybe a life built on ruins could still grow something sacred.

He walked through the village like a man unrecognizable—even to himself.

Past the tea stall.

Past the corner shop.

Past the eyes he had once feared would judge him.

And finally… to her street.

Belle was at the gate, towel slung over one shoulder, the evening sun turning her skin gold.

She wasn't expecting him.

When she saw the bag, her face broke—not into joy, not into panic—but into something raw and wordless.

Fear.

Hope. Disbelief.

He didn't say much.

Just stood there. And then, simply:

"I chose you." She didn't move.

Didn't cry.

Didn't speak.

But in the silence that followed, something sacred passed between them.

A contract without signatures.

A promise without conditions.

He had no future to offer.

No grand life to promise.

Only his truth. Only himself.

Not the version of him who lived in secrecy.

Not the man who loved her in whispers.

But the one who walked away from everything—

Just to stand in front of her.

CHAPTER 6
A FORCED MARRIAGE

Chapter 6: A Forced Marriage

It didn't happen without warning.

There was no thunder before the storm.

Just a quiet shift in Belle's voice—

A hesitation. A silence.

And then, a sentence that shattered everything:

"They've fixed my marriage."

Rumplestiltskin didn't speak.

He couldn't.

Because there are no words strong enough to hold back a wave that's already crashing.

He sat in silence, phone pressed to his ear, listening to the sound of her breath on the other end.

She wasn't crying. Not yet.

But he could feel it—like a scream curled up behind her ribs, waiting to break.

"They found a match," she said.

"Some relatives… from another town. His family came home yesterday."

Every word was a nail in the coffin of the life they had begun to imagine.

A quiet life.

A true life.

And now… it was being handed away in the name of tradition.

Belle didn't ask him to stop it.

She didn't beg.

Because she knew what he would've done if he could.

But what could he offer?

A man with no home.

No blessings.

No promise of safety.

Just a love that had no space in the world around them.

"I'm not ready," she whispered.

"But they're not asking."

The next few days moved like a funeral no one attended.

They didn't speak much.

He'd call and hear her voice cracking, not with emotion, but with exhaustion.

She had stopped fighting.

She was letting it happen—not out of choice, but out of surrender.

Because how many times can one girl say no before the walls

close in?

Rumplestiltskin watched from a distance as preparations began.

The mehendi. The gold. The forced smiles.

And Belle, shrinking inside herself.

He wanted to break down her door.

Drag her out of that house and into the future they once dreamed of.

But he had no legal right.

No blessing.

No force strong enough to carry her against the weight of a thousand expectations.

He sent her one final message before the ceremony:

"If I had the power, I'd be the man tying the thread around your neck.

But if I can't be him…

Then I promise—I'll be the one who never forgets who you really are beneath it."

She didn't reply.

On the day of her engagement, Rumplestiltskin walked aimlessly.

Through village paths.

Through memories.

Through pain so dense, even the earth beneath him seemed heavier.

She was being decorated in silk while his hands were empty.

She was being celebrated while he was being erased.

He didn't attend. He couldn't.

But he imagined her eyes—dry, distant, gone.

And he held onto one truth:

She didn't choose this.

And even if the world tied her to another man—

Her soul still remembered who she was before they took her away.

CHAPTER 7
THE RETURN

Chapter 7: The Return

She came back quietly.

No garlands. No celebration. No laughter trailing behind her.

Just the sound of footsteps that once ran toward him—

Now walking like they had forgotten how to belong.

Belle had returned to the village.

Rumplestiltskin heard about it from someone else.

Not from her.

The whispers floated through tea stalls and temple queues:

"She's back… the wedding didn't last… she's home again…"

He didn't believe it at first.

Because some wounds lie so deep, the idea of them healing feels impossible.

But then—he saw her.

From a distance.

Wearing the same kind of salwar she used to wear when they first met.

Hair tied back, eyes low, body slower.

Not broken.

But not the same.

They hadn't spoken in months.

Not since that message he sent—the one that said he would never forget who she really was.

Now she was walking toward the grocer's shop.

Hands empty.

Eyes tired.

He stood across the road, unmoving.

The world spun as usual—cattle carts creaked, motorbikes buzzed—but he was still.

Everything inside him stilled.

Belle didn't look at him.

Didn't wave.

Didn't falter.

But he knew she saw him.

Because her shoulders stiffened—like a violin string pulled too tight.

He didn't approach her.

He didn't dare.

That night, he waited outside the library bench where they used to meet.

Hours passed.

No sign.

Then just before the lights went out—he heard footsteps.

Soft. Familiar. Fragile.

She sat beside him.

Not close. Not distant.

Just there.

For a long while, neither of them spoke.

The wind carried old memories in fragments: the sound of her anklet, the echo of his laughter, the scent of jasmine that once braided her hair.

Then, finally—

"I'm not who I was," she said.

He turned to her, gently.

"I never expected you to be."

Belle looked ahead, not at him.

"They took something from me," she whispered. "And I let them."

She didn't cry.

She had no tears left.

"I thought I could forget," she continued. "I thought… if I wore the saree, smiled in the photos, obeyed their goddamn rules… I could survive."

Rumplestiltskin didn't interrupt.

This wasn't a conversation.

It was an unburial.

"But I wasn't living," she said. "I was folding myself into silence. Again. And again. Until I vanished."

A pause.

"And then one day… I woke up and didn't know whose life I was living anymore."

He swallowed the lump in his throat.

"I know," he said.

She finally looked at him.

Eyes older. Softer. Haunted.

"But you… you stayed the same."

He shook his head.

"No. I stayed here. That's different."

They both smiled.

Not happily.

But with the ache of two people who had carried the same storm, just in different directions.

She didn't ask to start again.

He didn't ask if she still loved him.

There was no promise made that night.

Only presence.

Only pain.

Only return.

CHAPTER 8
THE DIVORCE

Chapter 8: The Divorce

It didn't come with anger.

Not with shouting. Not with broken plates or doors slammed shut.

It came quietly—like the final exhale of a story that had run out of pages.

Rumplestiltskin stood outside the family court in town, wearing the same shirt he wore to his wedding.

It didn't fit the same anymore.

Neither did the life he was about to sign away.

The building was old, faded. The kind of place where dreams come to die in silence, notarized by strangers who never asked what love once felt like.

Inside, the clerk called his name.

He stepped forward.

The floor didn't crack.

The sky didn't fall.

But something inside him loosened—a thread tied too tightly for too long.

His wife sat across from him.

Not cold.

Not cruel.

Just done.

There was no fight left in her either.

Only a mutual understanding: this was over.

And maybe, it had been for years.

She didn't ask why.

She didn't ask who.

Because deep down, she already knew.

What hurt wasn't the betrayal.

It was the truth: that he had been gone long before she let him leave.

They signed the papers in silence.

No pen trembled.

No hands shook.

Just ink.

On paper.

Undoing years.

When it was done, Rumplestiltskin stepped outside.

It had started to rain again—soft and grey, like the sky was grieving without sound.

He didn't go home.

He didn't have one anymore.

Instead, he walked.

Through backstreets.

Through memories.

Past the tailor shop where Belle had once laughed.

Past the library bench where she had returned, older but still his.

He didn't call her.

Not yet.

Because divorce is not freedom.

It is grief with the door left open.

That night, he returned to a rented room above a clinic.

One fan. One bulb. One mattress on the floor.

He sat there, staring at the walls that didn't know his name, and let himself feel everything.

Guilt.

Relief.

Sadness.

Peace.

He hadn't left because he stopped loving his wife.

He had left because she had stopped being able to see him.

And somewhere else, someone else had.

The divorce didn't free him.

It just made space.

Space to finally show up—for Belle, for himself, for the version of life that didn't fit inside a lie.

He wasn't whole.

He wasn't healed.

But for the first time, he was honest.

And sometimes, that's all love really asks of us.

CHAPTER 9
MY PROMISE TO HER

Chapter 9: My Promise to Her

They didn't need words that day.

No questions.

No explanations.

Just a stillness between them that felt more intimate than touch.

They sat under the old banyan tree near the outskirts of the village.

The sky above was an early gold, fading gently into blue.

It was quiet — the kind of quiet that only two tired hearts could share.

Belle sat with her knees folded, head resting against the bark, eyes staring into nothing.

Rumplestiltskin sat beside her, a little distance away, unsure if he was allowed to close the space yet.

She hadn't spoken much since her return.

Not about the wedding.

Not about what had happened.

But he could see it.

In her face.

On the way she flinched when someone walked too close.

In the way she laughed now — if at all — with a kind of caution, like joy was something she no longer trusted.

She was here.

But not yet whole.

He reached into his shirt pocket and pulled out a tiny folded piece of paper.

Not a letter.

Just a promise.

He didn't give it to her.

He read it aloud.

Slowly. Softly. Like prayer.

"I promise…

to love the version of you that speaks, and the one that stays silent.

To hold you without asking why you're shaking.

To walk beside you, even when the world makes you walk with your head down.

To never ask you to forget — only to let me remember with you.

And when the day comes when you feel too small…

I promise to remind you who you were before they tried to erase you."

Belle turned her head, eyes wet.

Not from pain.

Not from fear.

But from recognition.

Someone had finally seen her grief not as a weight — but as something sacred.

She didn't say "I love you."

She didn't say "thank you."

She didn't have to.

Some moments live beyond language.

He didn't promise forever.

Because forever had already betrayed them once.

He promised to be there.

Patience.

Protection.

Not as a lover demanding love in return.

But as a man who knew what it meant to be broken — and what it meant to still believe.

Later that evening, as she walked away from the tree, she paused.

She turned. And for the first time since her return, Belle smiled.

Not wide.

Not loud.

But real.

And that was all the answer he needed.

CHAPTER 10

THE ENEMY WITHIN

Chapter 10: The Enemy Within

It's easy to fight the world.

Easier still to blame it.

Blame the village.

Blame her family.

Blame fate.

But the real war—the one that bleeds in silence—lives inside you.

Rumplestiltskin had done the impossible.

He had walked away.

Left behind a family, a home, a name.

He had chosen Belle. Chosen truth. Chosen himself.

And still…

He felt no peace.

Some nights, the guilt came like a shadow crawling up the wall.

He would lie awake on the thin mattress in that small rented room—fan spinning above, bare bulb flickering—thinking of the home he left.

Not the house.

The people inside it.

His daughters.

Their faces.

Their laughter echoing from memory into regret.

He remembered how one of them always clung to his hand when she slept.

How the other had a mole near her chin just like his mother did.

He remembered the tiny details.

And it killed him.

Not because he wanted to go back.

But because they hadn't deserved the version of him who had been too numb to stay.

Belle would visit sometimes.

Bring him food. Sit quietly.

She didn't ask what was wrong.

She knew.

He smiled when she was there.

He held her hand.

But even she could feel it—something distant, heavy, unsettled.

"You're still fighting it, aren't you?" she asked once.

He didn't deny it.

Because how could he?

There were nights when he missed his wife.

Not with longing.

But with guilt.

Not because he wanted her.

But because he had broken her.

And worse—because she hadn't tried to stop him.

He sometimes wished she had yelled.

Fought.

Begged.

Something.

But her silence had been the loudest scream.

And that echo lived inside him now.

One evening, while walking through the village, he caught his reflection in a shop window.

Not a mirror.

Just glass.

But enough.

He stopped.

I looked at the man staring back.

Not young.

Not strong.

Not certain.

Just… tired.

Tired of pretending he was okay.

Tired of carrying the weight of two lives.

Tired of punishing himself for being the one who left when all he ever wanted was to belong.

And for the first time since the divorce…

He cried.

Not the kind of tears you wipe away.

The kind you let fall.

The kind that hurts.

The kind that heals.

That night, Belle sat beside him as he wiped his face with the end of his shirt.

"I don't know how to forgive myself," he whispered.

Belle took his hand.

Pressed it to her chest.

"Then don't," she said.

"Just love what's left of you."

The enemy wasn't her family.

It wasn't his past.

It wasn't even the life he left behind.

It was the guilt.

The shame.

The weight of loving too hard in a world that doesn't know what to do with men who choose softness over survival.

But Rumplestiltskin was learning—slowly, painfully—

That sometimes, the bravest thing you can do…

I will stay.

Even when the enemy lives under your own skin.

CHAPTER 11
Gold, Lies, and Loyalty

Chapter 11: Gold, Lies, and Loyalty

It wasn't just love they were fighting for anymore.

It was survival.

Not from the village.

Not from judgment.

But from something colder, more dangerous—manipulation.

The first sign came when Belle's sister started asking questions.

Not curious ones.

Calculated.

"Why is he still around?"

"Don't you want a normal life?"

"Do you really think he'll give you a future?"

Belle didn't answer.

Because some truths were too sacred to throw into the middle of gossip.

But silence has its own cost.

It leaves space for others to speak on your behalf.

Then came the rumors.

Subtle.

Slick.

Slipping through doors, wrapped in sugar and poison.

They said Belle was being "kept."

That Rumplestiltskin was spending gold on her.

Gifts.

Trips.

Clothes.

That she was living off his pity, not his love.

None of it was true.

But truth never stands a chance against a well-dressed lie.

One day, Belle came to him — eyes tired, hands clenched, voice shaking with humiliation.

“They said you’re buying my loyalty.”

Rumplestiltskin stood silent.

Not because he agreed.

But because he had no idea how to fight lies that wore his name.

The pain wasn’t in the insult.

It was in the fact that the people closest to her—the ones who had watched her survive heartbreak—were now weaponizing that pain.

Turning her strength into shame.

Turning his love into control.

“I don’t need your gold,” Belle whispered.

He nodded.

"I know."

"I didn't stay because I was desperate."

"I know."

"I stayed because I saw myself in you."

His voice cracked.

"I know."

But not everyone wanted her to stay.

Not because of morality.

But because of money.

An old uncle hinted.

An elder cousin "advised."

A brother cornered her in the kitchen and offered her a new proposal — a wealthy man in the city. Clean slate. No past. More… respectable.

All they wanted was for her to choose security over love.

Image over truth.

And still, she chose him.

Day after day.

Lie after lie.

In rooms full of gold, she chose a man with nothing but scars.

One evening, she found him alone, sitting on the edge of the well where they once used to meet secretly.

He looked older.

Not in years.

But in grief.

"They won't stop," she said softly.

"I know," he replied.

"Then why are we still trying?"

He looked up.

Eyes swollen, but focused.

"Because love that doesn't survive a lie… was never loyal to begin with."

Belle didn't reply.

She just sat beside him.

And that night, without touching him, without saying a word—

She chose him again.

CHAPTER 12:
My Family's Wrath

Chapter 12: My Family's Wrath

Some wars are fought in silence. Others with screams.

But the worst ones… are fought at the dinner table.

Rumplestiltskin had chosen love.

But love, when it defies tradition, doesn't just break rules—it becomes a rebellion.

And every rebellion invites wrath.

The news of his departure had spread like wildfire.

It didn't need words. The empty bed. The quiet wife. The confused daughters.

Neighbors stared longer. Relatives whispered louder.

But it wasn't the world's judgment that shook him—it was his own blood.

It began with a phone call. His elder brother.

There was no greeting. Just a single line.

"You've shamed all of us."

Then came his mother.

Her voice was thin, like paper that had been folded too many times.

"I prayed for you every day," she said.

"But I didn't raise a man who would throw his family for… for what? A girl from nowhere?"

He didn't respond. Because no answer could hold enough weight to explain a heart that chose love over legacy.

Then came the visits.

An uncle knocked on his rented door—not to bring peace, but to drag guilt into his lap.

"You think love will feed you? Shelter you? Your wife stood by you for years. And this is what she gets?"

They didn't ask if he was happy.

They didn't ask if Belle was kind.

They didn't ask if he finally felt alive.

They only asked one thing:

"When will you come back and fix what you broke?"

But he didn't go back.

Not because he didn't care.

But because going back meant dying again.

Every word they hurled was not just anger—it was grief in disguise.

They weren't mourning his mistake.

They were mourning the version of him they had built in their minds.

And that version was gone.

One evening, Belle returned from the market, eyes red, silence heavy.

"They stopped me today," she whispered. "Your cousins. They

told me I ruined your name."

He clenched his jaw, but said nothing.

Because what could he say? That they were right?

That love—his love—had turned a quiet girl into the target of a village's rage?

She sat beside him, her voice barely a breath.

"Tell me something… was I worth it?"

And for the first time, he didn't rush to answer.

He simply reached out, held her hand, and said:

"No. You weren't worth it."

Her eyes widened.

He smiled softly.

"You were more."

That night, when the world felt too loud, they sat on the floor of their room, backs against the wall, fingers laced together.

The world was against them.

But in that moment, they had something stronger than acceptance—

They had each other.

And sometimes…

Love doesn't need to win the world.

It just needs to survive the war.

CHAPTER 13
STANDING ALONE

Chapter 13: Standing Alone

There comes a moment in every man's life when the echoes around him fade, and he realizes —

He is alone.

Not lonely.

But utterly… entirely alone.

Rumplestiltskin didn't expect applause when he chose love.

But he hadn't expected silence either.

Not this kind.

It was the kind of silence that lived in doorways left shut.

In phones that didn't ring.

In eyes that once held warmth, now filled with distance.

The village moved on.

It always did.

Its wells were still drawn from. Its festivals still lit the night sky.

But Rumplestiltskin…

He was no longer one of them.

He sat at the edge of the temple courtyard one morning, hoping to feel something sacred.

A place where he once prayed for peace — now only reminded him of the voices that had stopped calling his name.

Even the tea stall man, who used to slide him extra sugar, now served his cup without a word.

It wasn't hate.

It was worse.

He had become invisible.

Belle noticed.

She tried to shield him with softness — gentle touches, warm food, words laced with hope.

But even hope, when shared by two and crushed by a hundred, begins to wear thin.

"Why don't we leave?" she whispered one night.

"We'll go somewhere no one knows us."

He looked at her — the only light left in a darkening sky — and simply said:

"Because if I run now, I'll never stop running."

Standing alone wasn't a choice.

It was a necessity.

It was walking into the market and hearing laughter die when he passed.

It was watching Belle smile less, and speak softer.

It was knowing that to be with her… meant losing every other hand that once held him.

But it was also a strength.

The kind of strength that only grows when no one claps for your courage.

The kind that rises not from victory, but from persistence.

One evening, he stood on the rooftop, barefoot on the cool tiles, looking at the stars.

He remembered being a boy — looking up at the same sky — dreaming of a big life. A respected name. A family that praised him.

He got none of it.

But what he had now…

It was the truth.

Painful. Raw.

But honestly.

As Belle joined him, placing her hand in his, neither spoke.

They didn't need to.

Because some days, the bravest thing a man can do…

It stands.

Not with the crowd.

Not for a cause.

Just stand.

Alone.

And still choose love.

CHAPTER 14
HER SILENCE

Chapter 14: Her Silence

Some women scream when they're broken.

Some weep. Some run.

But Belle… She chose silence.

And that silence was louder than any storm Rumplestiltskin had ever known.

It began slowly.

She no longer asked if he ate.

She no longer touched his shoulder when he passed.

She sat beside him — yes — but like a ghost trying not to be seen.

The house wasn't filled with arguments or accusations.

It was filled with something worse:

Stillness.

At first, he told himself it was exhaustion.

She had faced enough — the stares, the whispers, the invisible weight of being the reason a man left his world behind.

Maybe she just needed space.

But space turned into distance.

And distance turned into walls.

Not made of bricks. Made of pauses. Of glances. Of the things she didn't say anymore.

One evening, Rumplestiltskin came home early with a bag of her favorite sweets.

He placed them on the table and waited for her smile.

It didn't come.

She didn't even look.

She simply folded clothes in silence — and that single sound of fabric rustling cut deeper than any fight.

He tried everything.

Long walks. Light jokes. Stories from his day.

Nothing reached her.

Until one night, under a dim yellow bulb, he finally asked:

"Have I lost you?"

Belle didn't look up.

She just whispered:

"No. I'm still here. But something in me isn't."

That broke him.

Because Rumplestiltskin had faced rejection before.

From society. From my family. Even from his own past.

But to be next to the woman he gave up everything for —

and still feel like a stranger —

was a loneliness he didn't know existed.

She hadn't stopped loving him.

But something in her had cracked — not because of what he did, but because of all she had to become.

She had been brave for too long.

Strong for too long.

And now, that silence wasn't punishment…

It was survival.

He stopped asking questions.

Instead, he did the dishes.

He refolded her clothes.

He sat beside her — not to fix her, but to simply let her be broken in peace.

Because some kinds of love don't shout.

They sit quietly.

They hold space.

They wait.

And Rumplestiltskin, the man who once moved mountains for love…

Now learned the hardest lesson of all:

Sometimes, the only way to hold on to someone…

Is to not hold too tightly at all.

CHAPTER 15
THE PROMISE I MADE TO AMMA

Chapter 15: The Promise I Made to Amma

Before Belle.

Before the betrayal.

Before the silence that stretched between him and the world—

There was Amma.

And some promises don't need to be spoken aloud.

They live beneath your skin, stitched between your ribs.

Rumplestiltskin sat alone in the room that once held her prayers.

The lamp she used still flickered in the corner.

The cot still creaked the same when he shifted weight.

She had been gone for years now.

But her absence was louder than ever.

Because now, more than ever, he remembered her voice.

"No matter where life takes you… never forget your dharmam."

Back then, he nodded.

Not understanding the weight of what she meant.

Now, her words sat on his chest like stone.

She had always been the quiet backbone of their family.

Not the loud one. Not the honored one.

But the one who carried their shame in silence.

Who covered their wounds without judgment.

And when he first told her — long ago — about the girl who made his heart burn again,

She didn't scold him.

She didn't bless it either.

She just looked at him with eyes that knew what it meant to be a woman waiting for a man who couldn't choose.

"Don't make her wait," Amma had whispered.

"And don't lie to the one who gave you children."

Back then, he hadn't listened.

Now…

He wished she were here to see that he finally understood.

Because it wasn't just love that broke his life.

It was delayed.

It was the cowardice of half-decisions.

Of staying too long in a place where no one was growing.

He had promised her something once.

That he would be a man she could be proud of.

That he wouldn't leave behind scars he couldn't repair.

But now, all he could see were the ruins of choices made too late.

One night, Belle found him in that room — staring at Amma's framed photo on the shelf.

"Is that her?" she asked.

He nodded.

"She would've liked you," he whispered.

And then corrected himself.

"Actually… I think she would've understood you."

Because Amma knew what it meant to hold in all your pain and still serve everyone tea with a steady hand.

Later that week, Rumplestiltskin lit a diya in her name.

No prayers.

No grand offerings.

Just a whisper into the dark:

"I know I failed you.

But I'm not done trying."

Some promises aren't about success.

They're about returning to who you were meant to be.

And for the first time in years…

Rumplestiltskin didn't feel like a runaway.

He felt like a son

Still trying to keep his mother's word.

CHAPTER 16:
Giving It All

Chapter 16: Giving It All

They say love is about giving.

But what they never say… is how much it takes from you first.

Rumplestiltskin had already given so much—his marriage, his name, his daughters, his place in the world.

And yet, it felt like he hadn't even started.

Because loving Belle wasn't just a decision.

It was a surrender.

They had moved into a small one-room rental on the edge of town.

No fan. No fridge. No promise of tomorrow.

Just cracked walls, two mugs, and each other.

At first, it felt romantic—like the rebellion was worth it.

Like they were rewriting their story from scratch.

But over time, the price began to bleed through the seams

He worked odd jobs. Manual labor. Field work. Sweeping godowns.

Anything that paid enough to bring back rice and tamarind.

He stopped buying razors.

Stopped meeting old friends.

Stopped expecting phone calls from anyone but his creditors.

And yet… every evening, when he walked home with aching bones and calloused hands, he would still look for her silhouette in the doorway.

And she was always there.

Silent.

Waiting.

Holding both his pride and his exhaustion in the same eyes.

One evening, Belle fell sick.

A fever. A shiver. Then vomiting.

There was no money for a hospital visit.

No help from the village that had already turned its back.

Rumplestiltskin sat beside her on the floor, pressing a damp towel to her head, whispering stories to distract her from the pain.

And in that dim light, watching her curl into herself, something in him snapped.

"Take everything," he whispered—not to anyone in particular.

To fate. To God. To whoever was listening.

"Take my health. Take my name. Just don't take her."

He pawned the last bit of gold he had—his father's ring.

The one he swore he'd keep till his grave.

He didn't even flinch.

Because some love stories aren't about how much you're willing to give…

They're about giving even when there's nothing left.

She recovered.

Slowly. Weakly. But she came back to him.

And when she did, she wept—not because of the pain, but because he never once asked her to be strong through it.

He simply held her weakness like it was holy.

People say real love is patient.

But that's only half the truth.

Real love?

Real love costs.

And Rumplestiltskin… had given it all.

CHAPTER 17
Writing Her Name on My Life

Chapter 17: Writing Her Name on My Life

Some people write names on paper.

Rumplestiltskin had written hers on his life.

He didn't know when it happened exactly.

It wasn't one moment—it was thousands of little ones.

A smile that broke his pain.

A silence that understood his chaos.

A hand that reached for his even when it trembled with shame.

It was a quiet evening.

The kind of evening when the air smells of burnt turmeric and laundry.

Belle sat cross-legged on the floor, brushing her damp hair with tired fingers, and he watched her—not like a lover, not like a husband, but like a man who had found God in a woman.

She didn't notice.

Because Belle never looked at herself the way he did.

He stepped into the room with a rusted old ink pen in hand—one he had kept since college, one that had once signed job applications and electricity bills.

Now, it had only one purpose.

He sat beside her, took her hand gently, and without a word, began writing on her wrist.

B-E-L-L-E

The letters weren't perfect. The ink bled. The lines trembled.

But the meaning didn't.

She looked at him, confused, then amused.

But then she saw his eyes—and the amusement melted.

He looked like a man who had just signed away the last piece of his soul.

"Why?" she whispered.

He didn't answer right away.

He simply held her wrist to his heart.

"Because everything else fades. But if I lose you… I want to carry you on me."

The next morning, she woke to find her name on a piece of cloth, stitched in red thread.

It was sewn into the inside of his only shirt.

Not where the world could see it—

But where it would rest against his chest.

She said nothing.

But that night, she tore a piece of her old school notebook and wrote his name in the corner.

Then I folded it.

And slipped it into her pillowcase.

They had no rings.

No rituals.

No photographs.

But they had each other's names hidden in the most sacred places.

And in a world that gave them no place to belong…

They wrote a love that no one could erase.

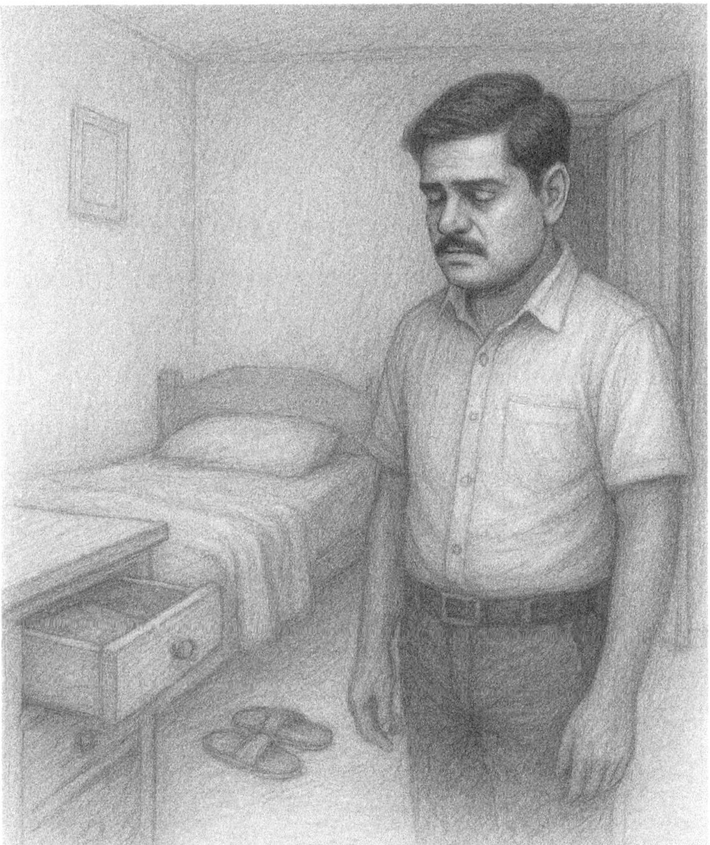

CHAPTER 18:
The Vanishing

Chapter 18: The Vanishing

It didn't happen all at once.

She didn't leave like a slammed door or a broken scream.

She vanished like steam from a morning cup—quiet, shapeless, inevitable.

Rumplestiltskin had stopped keeping track of time.

Days blurred into each other. Life became ordinary again—meals, laughter, silence, survival.

There were no big signs. No goodbye note. No suitcase by the door.

Just little absences.

A smile that didn't reach her eyes.

A moment too long at the window.

Phone calls she left the room to answer.

One afternoon, he came home early.

Belle wasn't there.

Her sandals were gone.

The drawer with her documents hung open.

The pillow she slept on was cold.

But it wasn't the emptiness of the room that broke him.

CHAPTER 19
Five Months of Darkness

Chapter 19: Five Months of Darkness

Time didn't move forward.

It collapsed.

Day by day, hour by hour, it folded in on itself—grinding Rumplestiltskin into dust that no one saw, no one missed, and no one tried to gather.

Belle was gone.

And he was still breathing.

But only because the body doesn't ask the heart for permission.

The first week, he refused to believe it.

"She must be with a relative," he told himself. "She'll come back once the storm settles."

But there was no storm.

Only a silence so complete it began to rot everything inside him.

The house turned hollow.

Not just empty, but haunted. Her laughter had soaked into the walls—and now it screamed through them in her absence.

Her towel still hung behind the door.

Her anklet still lay forgotten near the mat.

He didn't touch them.

He didn't dare.

Because removing her things would mean accepting she wasn't coming back.

Days turned into weeks.

He stopped working.

Stopped bathing.

Stopped answering calls.

Not because he didn't care, but because every ring that wasn't her made the world more unbearable.

He stayed up through nights, staring at the ceiling, begging for a sound—any sound—that could carry her voice.

Sometimes he thought he heard footsteps.

Sometimes he dreamed of her shadow.

Sometimes he called her name into the darkness, hoping the air would carry it to wherever she'd gone.

It never did.

The villagers began to talk again.

"Maybe she ran away."

"Maybe she used him."

"Maybe it was never real."

He didn't defend her.

Not because he agreed.

But because he didn't have the strength to speak.

What was the point?

Truth no longer lived in this world. It had died the day she disappeared.

One night, he walked to the bridge—the same one where he once waited hours just to see her pass by.

Now, it only held shadows.

He sat there until dawn, holding the stitched piece of cloth she once left in his shirt. Her name had faded.

But he still pressed it to his heart.

Just to feel.

Anything.

And then came the letter.

Folded in a temple donation box, placed by a hand he'd never known.

No name. No greeting.

Only five words:

"I had no other choice."

He read it a hundred times.

And every time… it broke differently.

Five months passed.

Five months where breath was punishment.

Where every rising sun felt like betrayal.

He had given up everything for her.

And yet—she was the one who left.

Not with hate.

Not with blame.

But with silence.

And somehow, that hurt more.

Because it meant she had loved him… and still walked away.

The world moved on.

Shops opened. Seasons changed. Festivals came and went.

But Rumplestiltskin stayed right there—frozen in the moment she left.

He didn't chase her.

He didn't hate her.

He simply stayed.

Because when you've built your whole world around someone…

There's no map back to yourself once they're gone.

And so he sat—heart half-alive, soul still whispering her name into a world that no longer answered.

Not hoping for a return.

Just remembering what it meant to feel.

Chapter 20
A Stranger's Marriage

Chapter 20: A Stranger's Marriage

He didn't ask for the truth.

But it came anyway.

Like betrayal dressed in silence.

Rumplestiltskin was sitting at a roadside tea stall, stirring sugar into a cup that had long gone cold. He wasn't waiting for anyone. He had stopped expecting anything. He existed now in a world suspended between denial and numbness.

Until someone tapped his shoulder.

"Hey… did you hear?"

Three words.

That's all it took.

He looked up, unsure if the voice was real. It was someone he vaguely recognized — a cousin, maybe. Or one of those half-friends who only show up when they carry something sharp.

"Hear what?" he asked quietly, his voice more breath than sound.

The man hesitated — only for a moment.

Then dropped a bomb in the shape of a whisper.

"Belle is married."

The world didn't spin.

It crashed.

Belle. Married.

The name alone had kept him alive for five months. And now it was being twisted, rewritten, rebranded with someone else's last name.

"She got married yesterday. A temple wedding. Simple. Very quiet."

He didn't want details.

But they came like poison without an antidote.

Her saree was red.

Her smile, tight and rehearsed.

Her new husband? A colleague from her office. Someone no one had mentioned before. A shadow from a place he never looked.

But none of that mattered.

Because it was hanging around her neck…

It was the thali he had bought.

The world inside him broke.

It wasn't just that she married someone else.

It was that she did it with the very chain he bought for her.

He remembered the day he purchased it — how his fingers trembled, how his heart raced with a dream of forever. He remembered how she cried when he showed it to her, whispering, "No one else will ever tie this on me."

She lied.

Or worse — she changed.

And now, that sacred symbol of his devotion had become her binding to another man. Another life.

Another story that didn't have him in it.

He left the tea shop without saying a word.

Not a scream.

Not a sob.

Just a man moving through air that felt like fire.

He walked through the streets as if gravity had loosened its grip on him. His limbs were heavy, his soul heavier. People laughed. Children ran past. The city moved on.

But he?

He was standing still in a moment that refused to end.

He reached home and opened the old metal box he had locked away—the one filled with pieces of her. A faded dupatta. A scribbled note. The earring she once left on his desk.

He touched each object like it was a landmine.

Because now, every piece of her was a weapon.

That night, he sat by the window.

Not waiting.

Not hoping.

Just… breathing.

In his hand was the ring he had planned to give her. A simple gold band. Nothing flashy. Just a promise.

Now, it was nothing.

He pressed it to his forehead, as if it could somehow take back time. But there was no time left.

Only aftermath.

Only the unbearable image of Belle—his Belle—smiling for a wedding photo beside a man who hadn't sacrificed his world for her.

Who hadn't fought through family, betrayal, and ruin.

Who hadn't lost everything just to keep her safe.

And yet…

He was the one who got her.

The tears came slowly.

Not loud.

Not dramatic.

Just quiet rivers on a face that had forgotten how to feel.

And then came the final breaking thought:

"She used the love I gave her… to build a life with someone else."

That truth was too cruel to hold.

But it was all he had left.

He didn't curse her.

Didn't hate her.

He just wept — for all the dreams that would never be born, for all the moments that were now someone else's memories.

Because when you give a woman your whole soul…

And she becomes a bride in a story you're not even part of…

You don't just lose love.

You lose yourself.

And no one tells you how to come back from that.

He left the tea shop without a word.

No scream. No sob. Just a man walking through air that burned.

The streets blurred past him. Laughter, footsteps, voices—life moved, but he remained trapped in a moment that refused to end.

At home, he opened the old metal box—her faded dupatta, a scribbled note, a single earring.

Each piece is once a treasure. Now, a blade.

That night, he sat by the window. Not waiting. Not hoping. Just breathing.

In his hand, the ring he had bought for her. A simple gold band. A promise unkept.He pressed it to his forehead. But there was no time left. Only aftermath.Belle—his Belle—now a bride beside a man who hadn't fought, hadn't bled for her.

And yet, he was the one who got her.

Tears came—not loud, not dramatic. Quiet rivers on a face that had forgotten feelings.

And the final, shattering thought:

She used the love he gave her… to build a life with someone else.

He didn't curse her. Didn't hate her. He wept—for dreams unborn, for moments stolen.

Because when you give a woman your whole soul, and she becomes a bride in a story you're not even part of—you don't just lose love.

You lose yourself.

And no one teaches you how to come back from that.

Chapter 21
The Man With My Chain

Chapter 21: The Man With My Chain

He didn't know the man's name.

But he didn't need to.

Because names don't matter when someone's wearing your chain.

Rumplestiltskin first saw him through a photo — a blurry image sent through a forwarded message, as cruel as it was uninvited. The stranger stood beside Belle, dressed in cream-colored silk, forehead dotted with sandal paste, the smile of a man who thought he had won.

But Rumplestiltskin didn't see a smile.

He saw theft.

Not just of a woman — but of a life.

A future.

A story that was written in blood and sacrifice and now rewritten with convenience and cowardice.

And around that man's neck… was his thali.

His sacred promise.

The one Belle had once kissed. The one she clutched to her chest with tears in her eyes saying, "Only you."

The one that had waited, just like him — in silence, in hope, in devotion.

And now, it was on another man.

Tied by another hand.

Claimed by someone who had no idea what it had cost.

He wanted to look away.

He wanted to forget.

But his eyes wouldn't move.

He studied the man — every detail. The way he stood too proud, too pleased. The way he held Belle's hand like a possession, not a prayer.

It wasn't jealousy.

It was grief.

Because Belle had once called Rumplestiltskin her temple, her home, her protector.

And now she stood beside someone who didn't even know the war she'd survived.

He hadn't wiped her tears. He hadn't held her broken. He hadn't built her from pieces.

But he was the one who got the ending.

Days passed.

But Rumplestiltskin couldn't let it go.

He had buried too many dreams, burned too many bridges, broken too many bonds — all for her.

And now, he was just a ghost in a love story he created.

He walked through the village like a man trying to forget how to breathe. Every face reminded him. Every whisper behind his back was a wound.

"They say she's happy."

"They say he's rich."

"They say she made the right choice."

And no one — no one — said he was the man who gave her everything.

One morning, he heard they were visiting the temple. The same one where he once prayed for her safety. Where he once begged the gods to keep her in his life.

He didn't plan to go.

But his feet moved before his mind did.

He stood near the stone pillars, hidden behind the crowd, watching.

There she was — Belle, in a green saree. Her hair in a braid. Her hand tucked beneath the arm of that man.

The man with his chain.

Rumplestiltskin didn't cry.

He didn't flinch.

He just looked.

And in that moment, something broke — not from pain, but from clarity.

She wasn't his anymore.

Maybe she never really was.

She wore his chain.

But she had given her heart… to a stranger.

And now, that chain was no longer sacred.

It was just metal around a neck that had never bent for love.

He turned around and walked away.

Not with anger.

Not with hate.

Just a man learning to live without the soul he once called home.

He didn't look back.

Because some stories don't need closure.

Some wounds never bleed out.

They just stay — quiet, permanent.

Like a chain you once gave in love…

Now worn by a stranger.

Chapter 22
The Truth That Broke Me

Chapter 22: The Truth That Broke Me

He didn't go looking for answers.

Because he already knew.

Somewhere deep down, in that quiet part of the soul that never lies — he knew.

But there's a difference between knowing and hearing it out loud.

And once he heard it, there was no going back.

It was a friend. A voice he trusted. A man who had once watched Rumplestiltskin and Belle share silence in a way that felt like prayer.

They met under a streetlamp, between two cups of tea and one unforgivable sentence.

"She was already seeing him," the friend said, voice low.

Rumplestiltskin didn't blink.

"What?"

"Back then. When you thought she was yours. When you fought your family. When you let your whole life fall apart for her…"

The words came like stones in his throat.

"She was already talking to him."

The world didn't just break.

It sank.

Like a ship that had been hollowed out long ago — and only now realized it had been carrying water this entire time.

Rumplestiltskin stood still.

Not because he was calm — but because his body didn't know how to move with this kind of pain.

His legs went numb.

His heart thudded so loud, even the traffic seemed to hush.

It wasn't just that she married someone else.

It wasn't even that she wore the chain he bought.

It was that…

She had loved him while loving someone else.

She had looked into Rumplestiltskin's eyes, held his hands, wept into his chest — all while sharing her smile with another man behind his back.

And that...

That truth didn't just hurt.

It unmade him.

He walked home that night like a shadow lost in the wrong world.

He opened his drawer — the one filled with her photos, her notes, the lipstick-stained tissue she once used and forgot on his table.

He stared at it all.

Every piece now felt fake.

Was any of it real?

The laughter?

The promises?

The night she cried saying she'd never leave?

Has it all been rehearsed?

Had he just been to the safe harbor… while she waited for the storm to pass?

He dropped to his knees.

The floor felt like it was made of knives.

And for the first time, he screamed.

Not out loud — not with his voice.

But with his soul.

A scream so deep that even silence bent to it.

A soundless roar that said:

"You didn't just leave me…

You lied to the version of me that loved you with his entire being."

He stared at the mirror.

The man who looked back wasn't broken.

He was erased.

Because betrayal doesn't always come with goodbye.

Sometimes, it comes dressed as love…

While holding another hand behind your back.

And the worst kind of heartbreak isn't when someone leaves.

It's when they were never really yours —

even while they said they were.

The next morning, the sun still rose.

The birds still sang.

But Rumplestiltskin didn't.

Because something inside him had died the night before.

Not his hope.

Not his love.

But something far more sacred.

His truth.

And once that breaks...

Nothing, and no one, can fix it again.

Chapter 23
I Still Would Have Said Yes

Chapter 23: I Still Would Have Said Yes

The world had taken everything from him.

His peace.

His name.

His sleep.

His future.

And now — even the truth had turned into something poisonous.

He had learned it all:

That she had loved another while claiming to love him.

That she had worn his chain… to marry someone else.

That every vow they shared was buried beneath a silence thick with secrets.

And yet…

If you asked him — even now, even here, after everything…

He would still whisper the same answer.

Yes.

He still would've said yes.

Yes, to the first message she sent with nervous hands.

Yes, for the first time she called him "mine."

Yes, for the first time she cried on his chest, and made him feel like love could heal broken men.

Yes, to every moment she made him believe this world could be beautiful again.

Because those moments, however temporary, were real to him.

And no truth — no betrayal — could erase the feeling of holding her like she was made of light.

Rumplestiltskin had stopped sleeping.

Not because he couldn't.

But because sleep meant peace — and peace belonged to people who didn't remember.

He remembered everything.

The curve of her voice.

The rhythm of her walk.

The way she'd rest her head on his shoulder, as if it had always belonged there.

And so he stayed awake.

Every night.

Haunted by ghosts that still smelled like jasmine and rain.

He once wrote her a letter he never sent.

It said:

"Even if I knew how this would end,

Even if you warned me you'd walk away…

I still would've chosen you.

A thousand times.

In every lifetime.

In every story.

Even if you weren't the ending —

You were still worth the beginning."

People asked him why he hadn't moved on.

He smiled.

They thought love was something you could pack away.

But real love?

It leaves bones behind.

He had bled for her.

Not just tears — but choices.

He gave her his name when she didn't ask.

Gave her a home when she didn't knock.

Gave her loyalty in a world where even memories weren't faithful.

And even now — even now — if she walked in that door, eyes wet and hands shaking…

He would fall to his knees and say it again.

Yes.

Not because she deserved it.

But because he meant it — even when she didn't.

That's what they'll never understand about Rumplestiltskin.

He didn't lose because she left.

He didn't lose because she lied.

He lost… because he loved for real.

And this world?

This world doesn't know what to do with men like that.

So every night, while others slept with dreams in their hearts, he sat by the window — heart in ashes, eyes to the stars — whispering a name that no longer answered.

Not in hope.

Not in regret.

Just in memory.

Because love, real love, doesn't beg to be returned.

It simply stays.

Quiet.

Unmoved.

Unshaken.

And even after the world burned every promise to the ground…

Rumplestiltskin whispered into the silence:

"I still would've said yes."

Chapter 24
A Thief in My Love

Chapter 24: A Thief in My Love

He didn't steal her with words.

Or with force.

He stole her in the quietest way possible —

by simply being there when Rumplestiltskin wasn't.

He didn't fight for her.

Didn't cry for her.

Didn't stand in front of fire or bleed in front of gods.

But he still got her.

Like a thief who waited in the shadows until someone else had built the temple…

and then walked in wearing the crown.

Rumplestiltskin had built that love with his own hands.

He had broken every rule for her.

Held her in her lowest.

Stood by her even when the whole world told him not to.

He gave her a home.

His name.

His future.

His life.

And the thief?

He gave her… nothing.

Except for timing.

He arrived when the story was broken.

And picked up the pieces like he had earned them.

But he hadn't.

Because this wasn't just a woman.

This was a life shared in whispers, scars, and promises.

It was a battlefield.

And the thief walked through it without ever lifting a sword.

People say you can't steal love.

But that's a lie.

Because you can stand in a life you didn't build,

and take credit for the peace someone else died to create.

That's what he did.

He put a ring on her finger.

Held her hand.

Called her his.

While Rumplestiltskin still had her name echoing in his blood.

One night, he saw them by chance.

Belle and the man who now carried his forever.

They were laughing.

Smiling.

Shopping for curtains.

Like love had never been a war.

Like no lives were ever sacrificed to keep it safe.

Like no man was ever stripped bare trying to protect it.

And it was then that Rumplestiltskin realized…

She didn't even tell the thief what he had stolen.

She handed herself over — wrapped in silence —

as if years of sacrifice didn't exist.

As if Rumplestiltskin had been nothing more than a shadow she walked past.

That night, he didn't cry.

Not because he didn't feel it.

But because there was nothing left to cry with.

He just stared at the ceiling, fists clenched, chest rising like it couldn't hold the fire anymore.

And at that moment, he wasn't broken.

He was robbed.

And no one saw it happen.

Because heartbreak makes noise.

But being replaced?

That happens in whispers.

If only the world knew…

That he still carried her voice in his bones.

That he still held on to the life they planned — even after she chose a different one.

That he still hadn't changed his phone number — just in case.

And the thief?

He would never know.

He would never know the girl Rumplestiltskin held when she fell apart.

Only the woman who stepped out was already rebuilt.

But Rumplestiltskin didn't hate him.

Because thieves don't know the value of what they steal.

They just take.

And love?

Real love?

It doesn't become hate.

It just becomes silent.

So Rumplestiltskin walked away — not because he was weak.

But because you don't fight someone…

for the life you already know you lost.

Chapter 25
Her Lies, My Loyalty

Chapter 25: Her Lies, My Loyalty

They say love makes you blind.

But Rumplestiltskin?

He wasn't blind.

He saw every red flag.

Every late reply.

Every secret glance at the phone.

Every time she said "I'm fine" when her eyes were clearly hiding something else.

He saw it.

He just chose loyalty over logic.

Because when you love someone enough… you don't leave at the first sign of danger.

You stay. You protect. You rebuild.

Even if it's killing you quietly.

He gave her everything.

Not just money.

Not just comfort.

A life.

He picked her up from rock bottom — when she had nothing.

He gave her dignity when the world mocked her.

He gave her dreams when she had forgotten how to sleep.

He made her feel like a queen when she didn't even know how to stand.

And in return?

She gave him lies, layered in sweetness.

Lies that tasted like trust.

Lies that sounded like promises.

Lies that looked like love…

until they turned into blades.

The betrayal wasn't just that she left.

It was how she left.

She didn't scream.

She didn't break things.

She simply walked out — while still holding everything he had built around her.

And worse?

She smiled as if nothing ever happened.

He had been loyal.

Through it all.

Through the tears.

The fears.

The nights she doubted herself.

The threats from her family.

The days he stood in front of demons wearing only his truth.

He fought for her when she wasn't even fighting for herself.

And in the end?

She handed his love to another man

wrapped in silence and stitched with deception.

They say the worst death is the one where your heart stops beating before your body does.

That's how he died.

Not in a hospital.

Not by accident.

Not from disease.

But from betrayal.

Quiet.

Surgical.

Unjust.

She killed him without a weapon.

Just a smile…

… and a lie.

He remembered one night — the night she called him crying.

Said she had no one.

Said she wanted to die.

He stayed on the call for 5 hours.

Talking her back to life.

Holding her through a phone line.

That night, he made a promise to himself:

"No matter how broken you get,

I will stay until you believe you deserve to live again."

And now?

She had erased all of that.

As if it was just a phase.

As if his loyalty was just a shadow she could step over.

But the truth?

The truth is… he still didn't hate her.

Even now.

Even after all the damage.

Because real loyalty doesn't end with betrayal.

It ends with grief.

And he grieved her like a widow at a funeral no one else showed up to.

He mourned the version of her that once held his hand like it was a lifeline.

He mourned the version of himself that still believed loyalty could save love.

People around him moved on.

They said, “She wasn’t worth it.”

They said, “You’ll find better.”

But no one saw the cost.

No one saw the years it took to build that loyalty.

No one saw the man who bled quietly… while giving someone a crown she wore only to run from.

He didn’t need closure.

He didn’t want revenge.

He just wanted one truth:

“I lied. And you didn’t deserve it.

You were the only one who never left.”

But she never said it.

And so, he kept walking with his silence…

And the world will never know

That the loudest love story in his heart…

Was the one that ended without justice.

Chapter 26
I Lost More Than Love

Chapter 26: I Lost More Than Love

Everyone thinks it was about the girl.

They see the tears, the silence, the broken promises —

and they say, "He lost the one he loved."

But that's not the truth.

He lost more than love.

Rumplestiltskin didn't just lose her.

He lost the man he used to be.

The one who believed in people.

The one who smiled without checking the room for danger.

The one who loved openly — without backup plans, without fear.

He lost the boy inside him who thought loyalty meant forever.

The boy who looked at love like it was sacred, not strategic.

He didn't just lose Belle…

He lost his world.

Before her, he had scars.

But he wore them with pride — proof that he had survived.

But after her?

He had wounds that didn't bleed.

Just burned.

Everywhere he went.

He stopped talking the same way.

Stopped laughing with his chest.

Stopped trusting when people said "I'll stay."

Because someone once said that too.

And now?

She was someone else's wife.

He didn't just lose a relationship.

He lost time.

Years.

Years of planning, dreaming, protecting.

He gave up his comfort.

His family.

His peace.

For what?

For someone who looked him in the eye…

and still lied.

The betrayal wasn't about another man.

It wasn't even about the wedding.

It was about all the truths she swallowed while he was still fighting for her.

It was about the way she walked out of a life he bled to build…

…like it was nothing.

He tried to rebuild himself.

I tried to go back to normal.

But the truth?

There's no "normal" after a loss like this.

Because you don't just lose a person.

You lose your reflection.

You lose the version of yourself who once believed you were enough.

He walks differently now.

Not slower. Not weaker. Just… quieter.

Like a man who knows life owes him no explanation.

Like a man who still carries a hundred "what ifs" in his pocket… but refuses to let them speak anymore.

And still, no one knows.

No one sees.

That when Rumplestiltskin smiles today,

It's not happiness.

It's a memory.

It's a man trying to remember what it felt like to be someone worth staying for.

So no…

He didn't just lose love.

He lost parts of himself no one clapped for.

No one mourned.

No one came looking.

But they're gone.

And he feels they are missing… every day.

Chapter 27
Still I Wait

Chapter 27: Still I Wait

Time doesn't heal.

It hides.

It buries.

It distracts.

But healing?

Healing never came.

Everyone said, "Move on."

"You deserve better."

"She doesn't deserve you."

And yet…

Every morning, before the world wakes —

Rumplestiltskin still looks at the door.

Not to open it.

Not to chase her.

Just… to see if today is the day it opens on its own.

Because deep down —

where even grief doesn't go —

he still waits.

He waits for her to say,

"I made a mistake."

He waits for her to whisper,
"I miss you every single day."
He waits for an apology
that never learned how to travel back in time.
Some days, he hates her.
But most days?
He misses her more than he misses himself.
And that's the cruelest part.
He doesn't even know who he is anymore.
But he still remembers
the sound of her laugh against his chest.
He doesn't count time in months anymore.
He counts it in missed calls
and silent prayers she'll never hear.
In the weight of words he never got to say.
In the ghost of the wedding he imagined every day.
He waits…
in places they used to sit.
on the streets they used to walk.
under skies that once heard them dream.
And it's not hope.
He doesn't wait because he thinks she'll come back.

He waits because some hearts don't know how to stop.

Because some loves don't end with goodbye.

They echo.

Forever.

People moved on.

Friends forgot.

Families healed.

The world spun forward.

But Rumplestiltskin?

He remained in the pause.

That moment when everything shattered —

and nothing was ever the same again.

He once told her,

"Even if you leave me…

I'll still believe in you."

And he meant it.

Because love, to him,

was never a transaction.

It was devotion.

Even if it meant bleeding silently forever.

So now?

He still wakes at 3 a.m.,

hoping for a message that never arrives.

He still checks her last seen.
Still hears her voice in his sleep.
Still rewrites memories,
wondering which smile was real
and which was rehearsed.
And even after all of this...
He doesn't regret loving her.

He only regrets one thing:
That he loved her alone at the end.
"Still I wait,"
he whispers to the air.
Not because she deserves it.
Not because she'll return.
But because when you love someone that deeply...
There's no off switch.
There's only silence.
And the man who still listens for her in it.

Chapter 28
The Day I Let Her Go (But Didn't Stop Loving Her)

Chapter 28: The Day I Let Her Go (But Didn't Stop Loving Her)

Letting go is supposed to bring freedom.

But for Rumplestiltskin,

It felt like death with no funeral.

He didn't scream.

Didn't break things.

Didn't beg.

He simply stood there —

as the truth wrapped around his heart

and squeezed until he couldn't feel it beat anymore.

She had chosen her life.

And he?

Choose her happiness over his existence.

He told himself it was time.

That he had to stop waiting.

That she had already left — in body, in silence, in truth.

But when your soul is still holding her name like a prayer…

How do you tell it to forget?

So that morning, he did the hardest thing he's ever done.

He let her go.

He opened his hands — the same ones that once shielded her from storms —

and allowed her memory to slip through like dust.

But it wasn't peaceful.

It was a war.

A war inside him where every version of himself screamed not to do it.

He deleted her number.

Blocked her profile.

Burned the letters.

Erased the playlists.

But no matter how hard he tried…

He couldn't delete the parts of her stitched into his soul.

He remembered everything.

The first smile.

The rain-kissed conversations.

The way she rested her head on his shoulder like it was her favorite place in the world.

And he knew —

Those moments would haunt him for the rest of his life.

Not as regrets.

But as proof that he once loved without boundaries.

Letting go wasn't the end of love.

It was the beginning of loving her silently.

Without hoping.

Without expecting.

Without needing her to know.

He imagined her smiling somewhere.

With someone else.

He pictured her living the life he once planned for her.

And it hurts.

But beneath the ache… was something deeper.

Pride.

Because he had given her that life.

Not the man she was with now.

Not her family.

Not fate.

Him.

He was the architect of her happiness —

and she would never even say his name when people asked how she made it.

He walked away.

Not because he stopped loving her.

But because she had already walked away from him —

emotionally, spiritually, completely.

And sometimes,
real love isn't holding on.
It's choosing to hurt
so the person you love doesn't have to.
He still dreams of her.
Still whispers "take care" into the night.
Still tears up when he hears her favorite song.
But no one sees that anymore.
Because now?
His love lives in silence.
And that's the truth.
The day he let her go…
He didn't stop loving her.
He just stopped showing it.
Because real love?
It doesn't always look like forever.
Sometimes…
It looks like goodbye.

Chapter 29
When Memories Beg Me Not to Forget Her

Chapter 29: When Memories Beg Me Not to Forget Her

He tried to forget.

God knows he tried.

He changed his routine.

Deleted her photos.

Stopped visiting the places they once called forever.

But memory?

It doesn't listen.

Some nights, it whispers her name.

Not in anger.

Not in regret.

But in longing.

As if it, too, can't live without her.

Rumplestiltskin doesn't cry as often now.

But when he does, it's not from fresh wounds.

It's from the scars that still ache — years later

From the memories that beg him,

"Please don't erase her. Not yet."

He finds her in the smallest things.

A jasmine flower outside the temple.

A song in a passing auto.

A towel hung behind a bathroom door.

Every moment says,

"She was here."

Every silence says,

"She should be."

He doesn't fight the memories anymore.

Because every time he tries to let go,

they hold tighter.

Like they're afraid

that forgetting her would mean

she never mattered.

And that?

That hurts worse than anything.

He kept one photo.

Tucked deep in a book no one touches.

Her eyes looked into his like she used to.

Soft.

Shy.

Certain.

Back when love wasn't complicated —

just true.

And some nights,

He opens it like a wound.

He doesn't talk.

Just… remember.

Because memories are all he has now.

No replies.

Not presence.

Just echoes of a love that shook his soul.

People think forgetting is healing.

But what if memory is the only place

where she still loves him back?

What if forgetting

means burying the only version of her

Was that ever truly his?

So he keeps remembering.

Not because it helps.

Not because it hurts.

But because of those memories?

They beg him not to let go.

They plead —

with every scent, every sound, every stillness:

"Keep her alive in you.

If you let go… we disappear too."

Rumplestiltskin knows she's gone.

Gone in body.

Gone in choice.

But never gone in memory.

And when he sleeps?

He prays not for dreams without her —

but for the ones where she still reaches for him.

Where time bends,

and she never leaves.

Where love doesn't end in silence.

Where memory is not punishment…

…but mercy.

Chapter 30
The Love I'll Carry Into My Next Life

Chapter 30: The Love I'll Carry Into My Next Life

Some love stories end.

Some fade.

Some shatter quietly in the middle of a crowd.

But not this one.

This one

will live beyond lifetimes.

Rumplestiltskin wasn't just a man who lost love.

He was a man who became love.

In its rawest, most painful, most faithful form.

Even when she walked away.

Even when silence replaced words.

Even when she married someone else wearing the chain he had once bought…

He still loved her.

Not because he was weak.

But because his love was pure.

The kind of love that doesn't need a return.

That doesn't expire with betrayal.

The kind that writes books like this.

He once believed they would grow old together.

He dreamt of building a life.

Of kids who looked like her.

Of mornings with her smile,

and nights with her head resting on his chest.

But fate?

It had other plans.

Plans that didn't just steal her —

They stole his future.

And yet…

He forgave.

Not because she asked.

But because real love doesn't keep scores.

It keeps space in the soul — for the one it can never replace.

Now, as the story ends…

He doesn't claim to have healed.

He doesn't say he's fine.

But he has accepted.

Accepted that she was the storm and the shelter.

The wound and the reason he still breathes.

And if there is another life —

another sunrise

in another body

another time…

He knows one thing:

He will love her again.

All over again.

From the beginning.

He hopes she'll remember him in the next world.

Maybe her soul will pause when he walks past.

Maybe she'll recognize that ache —

the one only he ever knew how to soothe.

Maybe in that life,

she'll choose him.

Completely.

Without fear.

Without betrayal.

And maybe then…

The love he carried across lifetimes

will finally come home.

Until then?

He lives quietly.

Softly.

Still loving her

with the kind of devotion gods write destinies around.

To the world, he may look like a man who lost.

But those who feel deeper?

They know the truth:

He was the man who loved —

so deeply,

so endlessly,

so honestly…

that even Time couldn't forget him.

This isn't a goodbye.

This is a promise.

"I'll meet you again.

In a world where love doesn't lose.

And hearts don't break quietly."

"And when I do...

I'll love you like I never stopped."

"This is the final image of a man who never stopped loving – even when the story ended."

Closure Note

She may forget me.

But I will remember her — in this life,

and in every life to come.

And if there is another life —

I'll still carry her with me, still.

But this time,

I hope she remembers me too.

About the Author

Raghavan Adhisankar is a businessman, writer, and a man who once chose love over everything — and paid the price.Born in Indai. he built a life of responsibility and resilience. But one love changed him forever.Loved Her Enough to Lose Myself is not just his debut novel — it is his truth, written with raw honesty and an unflinching heart.Today, Raghavan continues to run his businesses and quietly carry the memories of a love that shaped him.

This is his story — and perhaps, yours too.

www.ingramcontent.com/pod-product-compliance
Lightning Source LLC
Chambersburg PA
CBHW062139160726
48282CB00027B/877
9789334327540